The Lion, the Witch and the Wardrobe

C.S. LEWIS

Illustrated by **Christian Birmingham**

HarperCollins *Children's Books*

To Louise, Alice, Rory and Sam

The illustrator would also like to thank
George H-H, Douglas Gresham, Gerry, Danielle,
Christian, Jo and Daniel at Looe Comunity School
and Katrina Flanagan at the Irish Tourist Board
for their help.

A percentage of the royalties from this
book goes to the Born Free Foundation,
Coldharbour, Surrey RH5 6HA.

This edition published 2010

First published in Great Britain by HarperCollins*Publishers* Ltd 1998

Adapted from *The Lion, the Witch and the Wardrobe* copyright © C. S. Lewis Pte Ltd 1950
Abridged by Amanda Benjamin
Abridged text copyright © C. S. Lewis Pte Ltd 1998
Illustrations copyright © Christian Birmingham 1998

ISBN 978 0 00 774379 7

The illustrator asserts the moral right to be identified as the illustrator of the work.

The Chronicles of Narnia®, Narnia® and all book titles, characters and locales
original to The Chronicles of Narnia are trademarks of C.S. Lewis Pte. Ltd.
Use without permission is strictly prohibited.

A catalogue record for this book is available from the British Library.

Printed in China by South China Printing Co., Ltd

Once there were four children called Peter, Susan, Edmund and Lucy. They were sent away from London during the Second World War, to the house of a kind old Professor who lived in the country.

On the first morning the children decided to explore the big house. It was full of interesting things and unexpected places. One room had a suit of armour in it. Another, all hung with green, had a harp in the corner. And one room was quite empty except for a big wardrobe with a looking-glass in the door.

"Nothing there," said Peter, and they all trooped out again – all except Lucy.

Opening the wardrobe door, she saw several long fur coats hanging up, and immediately got in amongst them. As she went further in, she noticed to her surprise that the soft furs began to feel rough and prickly, just like the branches of trees.

A moment later Lucy was standing in the middle of a wood with snow under her feet and snowflakes falling through the air.

Lucy felt a little frightened, but very excited too. Ahead of her, between the dark tree trunks, a light was shining. She walked towards it, *crunch-crunch* over the snow. It was a lamp-post. As Lucy stood wondering why there was a lamp-post in the middle of a wood, she heard a pitter-patter of feet, and then a very strange person stepped out from among the trees.

From the waist upwards he was like a man, but his legs were shaped like a goat's. He had a pleasant little face and curly hair, out of which stuck two horns. He was a faun. When he saw Lucy he gave a start of surprise.

"Good evening," said Lucy.

"Good evening," said the Faun. "Excuse me – but are you a Daughter of Eve?"

"My name is Lucy," she said, not quite understanding him.

"But – forgive me – are you what they call a girl?" he asked.

"Of course I am," replied Lucy, thinking his questions very strange.

"I have never seen a Son of Adam or a Daughter of Eve before," said the Faun. "I am delighted to meet you. My name is Tumnus."

"I am very pleased to meet you, Mr Tumnus," said Lucy.

"And may I ask, O Lucy Daughter of Eve," said Mr Tumnus, "how you have come into Narnia?"

"Narnia? What's that?" said Lucy.

"This is the land of Narnia," said the Faun. "Everything that lies between the lamp-post and the great castle of Cair Paravel on the eastern sea."

"I got in through the wardrobe in the spare room," said Lucy.

"Ah!" said Mr Tumnus. "If only I had worked harder at geography when I was a little faun, I should know all about these strange countries."

"But they aren't countries at all," said Lucy, almost laughing. "It's only just back there – it is summer there."

"Meanwhile," said Mr Tumnus, "it is winter in Narnia, and has been for ever so long, and we shall both catch cold if we stand here talking in the snow. Daughter of Eve from the far land of Spare Oom, would you like to come and have tea with me?"

"I'd like that very much," said Lucy, who was feeling quite hungry. "But I won't be able to stay long."

And so Lucy found herself walking through the wood arm in arm with the Faun as if they had known each other all their lives.

They had not gone far when Mr Tumnus led Lucy into a little cave, where a wood fire burned merrily. Lucy thought she had never been in a nicer place.

For tea there was a nice brown egg each, sardines on toast, toast with honey, and finally a sugar-topped cake.

The Faun told Lucy wonderful tales of life in Narnia – about midnight dances with the wood nymphs and water sprites, about the milk-white stag who would give you wishes if you caught him, and treasure-seeking with the Red Dwarfs.

Then he took up a little flute and played a tune that made Lucy want to cry and laugh and dance all at the same time. Finally she said, "Oh, Mr Tumnus – I'm sorry to stop you, but really I must go home."

To her surprise, the Faun's brown eyes filled with tears.

"Oh – oh! I'm such a bad Faun," he sobbed.

Lucy put her arms around him and gave him her handkerchief. "No, you're not," she said. "You are the nicest Faun I've ever met. But what have you done?"

"I'm in the pay of the White Witch," Mr Tumnus wept. "It is she that has Narnia under her thumb and makes it always winter. Always winter and never Christmas, think of that!"

"How awful!" said Lucy. "But what does she pay *you* for?"

"That's the worst of it," said Mr Tumnus with a groan. "I had orders from her that if I ever saw a Son of Adam or a Daughter of Eve I was to catch them and hand them over to her."

"Oh, but you won't, will you, Mr Tumnus?" said Lucy anxiously.

"If I don't," he replied, "she'll wave her wand and turn me into stone so that I will be a statue in her horrible house."

"I'm very sorry, Mr Tumnus," said Lucy. "But please let me go home."

"Of course I will," said the Faun. "I can't give you up to the Witch, not now that I know you. But we must be off at once. The whole wood is full of *her* spies." So they hurried through the darkness, back to the lamp-post.

"Go home as quickly as you can," said the Faun, "and can you ever forgive me for what I meant to do?"

"Why, of course I can," said Lucy. "And I do hope you don't get into trouble on my account."

"Farewell, Daughter of Eve," said Mr Tumnus. "Perhaps I may keep the handkerchief?"

"Of course! Goodbye!" called Lucy, running toward the wardrobe door. Soon, instead of rough branches brushing past her she felt soft coats, and all at once she was stepping out into the empty spare room.

Lucy ran into the hall, where Peter, Susan and Edmund were still standing.

"I'm here," she shouted. "I've come back, I'm all right."

"What are you talking about, Lucy?" said Susan, for to them no time had passed at all.

Lucy told them excitedly that the wardrobe was a magic one. "There's a wood inside it, and it's snowing, and there's a faun and a witch. It's called Narnia. Come and see!"

The others did not know what to think, and followed her back into the room. But when Susan pulled the fur coats apart, all they saw was the back of the wardrobe with hooks on it. Peter rapped his knuckles on it to make sure that it was solid.

Poor Lucy couldn't understand it at all, and the others simply thought she was making it all up.

The next wet day the children decided to play hide-and-seek. Lucy went at once to the wardrobe. She wanted to have one more look inside it, for she was beginning to wonder whether Narnia hadn't been a dream.

Meanwhile Edmund, who could be quite spiteful, secretly followed Lucy to tease her about her imaginary country. He came into the room just in time to see her vanishing inside the wardrobe.

Jumping in after her, Edmund closed the door behind him, forgetting what a silly thing this is to do. To his astonishment he found himself in the middle of a snowy wood.

Lucy was nowhere to be seen, and everything was perfectly still, as if he were the only living creature around.

Then Edmund heard a sound of bells. It came nearer and nearer. Moments later a sledge swept into sight, driven by a fat dwarf. Behind him sat a great lady covered in white fur up to her throat. She held a long straight golden wand in her hand and wore a golden crown. Her face was white like snow, beautiful and proud.

"Stop!" ordered the Lady. "And what, pray, are you?"
she asked, looking hard at Edmund.

"I'm – my name's Edmund," he replied.

The Lady frowned. "Is that how you address a queen?" she asked sternly. "But I repeat – what *are* you? An overgrown dwarf?"

"No, I'm a boy, your Majesty," said Edmund.

"A Son of Adam," hissed the Queen, and raised her wand.

Just as Edmund thought she was going to do something dreadful, she suddenly said in quite a different voice, "My poor child, how cold you look! Come and sit with me."

Edmund dared not disobey. So he stepped on to the sledge and the Queen wrapped her warm fur mantle around him.

"Now, what would you like best to eat?" she asked.

"Turkish Delight, please, your Majesty," said Edmund.

The Queen took out a small bottle and let one drop fall on to the snow. Instantly there appeared a box of Turkish Delight. Edmund had never tasted anything more delicious in his life.

While he was eating, the Queen asked him questions. She got him to tell her that he had a brother and two sisters, and that one of his sisters had already been in Narnia and met a faun.

At last the Turkish Delight was finished. Edmund wished he could have some more. He did not know that the Turkish Delight was enchanted, and that anyone who had once tasted it would want more and more of it.

The Queen knew quite well what Edmund was thinking, but instead of offering him any more, she said, "Son of Adam, I should so much like to meet your brother and your two sisters. Will you bring them to see me? Because if you did come again, you could eat Turkish Delight all day long. I have no children of my own, and as you are the cleverest and handsomest young man I've ever met, I think I would like to make you the Prince of Narnia."

Then she pointed with her wand. "You have only to look for those two hills rising above the trees and walk towards them to reach my house. But remember – you must bring the others."

"I'll do my best," agreed Edmund.

"You needn't tell them about me," said the Queen. "It would be fun to keep it a secret between us two. Make it a surprise for them!"

As the sledge swept away, she called, "Don't forget. Come soon!"

Edmund was still staring after it when he heard Lucy calling him.

"Oh, Edmund! So you've got in too!" she cried. "I've been having lunch with dear Mr Tumnus, and the White Witch has done nothing to him, so he thinks she can't have found out."

"The White Witch?" said Edmund. "Who's she?"

"She is a perfectly terrible person," said Lucy. "She calls herself the Queen of Narnia, though all the fauns and nymphs and animals hate her. She can turn people into stone and she has put an enchantment on Narnia so that it is always winter."

When he heard that the Lady he had made friends with was a dangerous witch, Edmund felt very uncomfortable. But he still wanted to taste that Turkish Delight more than anything else.

By this time they had walked a good way. Then suddenly they felt coats around them instead of branches and next moment they were both standing outside the wardrobe in the empty room.

"Come on," said Lucy, "let's find the others. What a lot there is to tell them!"

But when Lucy told Peter and Susan that Edmund had been in Narnia too, he suddenly decided to do a very spiteful thing and said, "Oh, yes, Lucy and I have been playing – pretending that her story about a country in the wardrobe is true. Just for fun, of course. There's nothing there really."

Poor Lucy gave Edmund one look and rushed out of the room.

Now, sightseers often came to see the professor's interesting old house. The children usually kept out of their way, but one morning, a few days later, they just couldn't seem to avoid them.

"Here – let's hide in the Wardrobe Room," said Susan. But once inside, they heard voices at the door.

"Quick!" said Peter, and flung open the wardrobe. They all bundled inside – and suddenly found themselves surrounded by snow-covered trees.

"Why, we've got into Lucy's wood!" said Peter. He turned at once to her. "I'm sorry for not believing you, Lu."

"That's all right," she said. "Let's go and see Mr Tumnus. He's the nice Faun I told you about." So, each borrowing a fur coat, they set off.

But at the Faun's cave a terrible surprise awaited them. The door had been wrenched off its hinges and everything lay smashed on the floor. Nailed to the carpet was a note. It said that Mr Tumnus had been arrested for high treason against the Queen of Narnia.

"She isn't a real queen at all," cried Lucy. "She's a horrible witch, and all the wood people hate her. Oh, we must try to rescue him."

"Look!" cried Susan suddenly. "There's something among the trees."

The whiskered, furry face of a beaver peeked out at them.
"Are you the Sons of Adam and Daughters of Eve?"
it whispered, and to show it was a friend,
the Beaver took out the handkerchief
Lucy had given Mr Tumnus.

"Poor fellow, he said that if anything happened to him I must meet you here," the Beaver told them. Then it added, "Aslan is on the move."

Now, none of the children knew who Aslan was, but at his name each of them felt something jump inside. Peter felt brave and adventurous. Susan felt as if beautiful music had just floated by, and Lucy got the feeling you have at the beginning of summer. But Edmund felt only mysterious horror.

"And what about Mr Tumnus?" said Lucy. "Where is he?"

"Shhh, not here," said the Beaver. "I must bring you where we can have a real talk."

So they all hurried along behind their new friend and presently came to a large frozen river. A dam had been built across it, and on top of the dam was a little house.

But Edmund also noticed two small hills in the distance, and was sure that the White Witch's palace lay between them.

Mrs Beaver was waiting for them, and in no time the children were seated round a table eating freshly caught fish and boiled potatoes with plenty of butter.

"And now," said Mr Beaver when they had all finished eating, "we can get to business. First of all, Mr Tumnus has been taken to the Queen's house and turned into stone. There's nothing any of us could do on our own, but now that Aslan is on the move..."

"Oh, yes! Tell us about Aslan," they all cried.

"Aslan? Why, he's the King!" said Mr Beaver. "He's the great Lion and the Lord of the whole wood, but not often here, you understand. Now, word has reached us that he's come back to Narnia, and you are to meet him tomorrow at the Stone Table.

"He'll settle the White Witch all right. For there's an old saying that when Aslan returns and two Sons of Adam and two Daughters of Eve sit in the four thrones at Cair Paravel, then it will be the end not only of the White Witch's eternal winter but of her life.

"That's why she wants to get you all to her castle, where she can turn you to stone, and so rule Narnia for ever!"

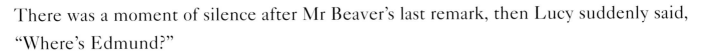

There was a moment of silence after Mr Beaver's last remark, then Lucy suddenly said, "Where's Edmund?"

Everyone rushed to the door and looked out. Snow was falling thickly and steadily, but Edmund was nowhere to be seen.

"He will have gone to the White Witch," said Mr Beaver grimly. "I thought he looked as if he was under her enchantment. We must go to the Stone Table at once, before the Witch catches us! There's not a moment to lose."

Edmund was indeed making his way to the White Witch's house.

After a long and bitterly cold walk through snowy, icy drifts, he came to it at last. The iron gates stood wide open, and he made his way cautiously through a courtyard filled with stone statues.

Across the threshold lay a great wolf. It rose, the hair bristling along its back, and growled, "Who's there?"

"If you please, sir," said Edmund, trembling, "I'm the boy that her Majesty met in the wood the other day."

The Wolf vanished into the house and Edmund followed.

"How dare you come alone!" cried the Witch in a terrible voice.

"I've brought the others quite close, your Majesty," stuttered Edmund. "They're with Mr and Mrs Beaver."

A cruel smile came over the Witch's face – until Edmund told her all he had heard before leaving the Beavers' house.

"What! Aslan?" cried the Queen, and clapped her hands. Instantly the dwarf appeared.

"Make ready our sledge," she ordered.

In the meantime, Mr and Mrs Beaver were leading the children along the river bank.

At last, when Lucy was so tired that she was almost asleep on her feet, they came to a snug little hole where they could spend the night.

They awoke to the sound of jingling bells.

Mr Beaver was out of the cave like a flash. Then they heard him shout, "It's all right. Come out, everyone. It isn't *her*!" They all scrambled up the steep bank. There, on his sledge, sat Father Christmas, big and glad.

"I've come at last," he said. "The White Witch has kept me out for a long time, but her magic is weakening. Aslan is on the move! And now, for your presents," he smiled.

"Mrs Beaver, a new sewing machine is waiting for you at home, and Mr Beaver, you will find your new dam quite finished."

The kind creatures were so pleased they could hardly speak.

Then Father Christmas gave Peter a magnificent sword and shield. For Susan there was a bow and a quiver of arrows, and a little horn. Last of all, he gave Lucy a clear crystal bottle and a small dagger.

"In this bottle," he said, "there is a cordial made of the juice of the fire-flowers. If you or any of your friends is hurt, a few drops of this will restore them." Then he cried out, "Merry Christmas! Long live the true King!" and drove out of sight.

"It is time we too were moving on," said Mr Beaver.

Edmund meanwhile had been having a horrible time. When he asked the White Witch for Turkish Delight, she merely said, "Silence, fool!" and as they sped through the darkness, he felt colder and more miserable than ever before in his life. It didn't look now as if she intended to make him a king, and he longed to be with the others.

At last morning came, and they were travelling along in daylight.

Suddenly the Witch stopped the sledge. Nearby sat a merry party celebrating the return of Father Christmas. In fury the Witch turned them all to stone, and Edmund for the first time felt sorry for someone besides himself.

As they raced on again, Edmund noticed that he was feeling much less cold. Soon patches of green began to show through the snow.

The sledge gradually came to a halt and the Witch ordered them to leave it behind and walk. When Edmund heard birds singing his heart leapt, for he realised that the Witch's cruel winter was over.

Miles away, the other children were walking into what seemed a delicious dream, through warm sunlight into green thickets and mossy glades.

"Not long now," said Mr Beaver, and began leading them up a hill.

At the top of it stood the Stone Table, and nearby all sorts of wonderful creatures were gathered around Aslan himself – centaurs and unicorns, wood nymphs and water sprites, deer and great birds.

The children could hardly look into the Lion's royal, solemn eyes, for he was both good and terrible at the same time.

Finally Peter stepped forward and said, "We have come, Aslan."

"Welcome, Peter, Son of Adam," said Aslan. "Welcome, Susan and Lucy, Daughters of Eve. Welcome, He-Beaver and She-Beaver." His voice was deep and rich. "But where is the fourth?"

"He has betrayed them and joined the White Witch," said Mr Beaver.

"Please, Aslan, can anything be done to save Edmund?" said Lucy.

"All shall be done," said Aslan. Then he said to Peter, "Come, Son of Adam, and I will show you the castle of Cair Paravel, for you are the firstborn and will be High King of Narnia over all the rest."

Below them in the evening light,
where Narnia met the sea, the
castle shone like a great star.
Suddenly a noise broke the silence.

"It is your sister's horn," said Aslan.

Running towards the sound, Peter saw creatures scattering in every direction.
Then he saw Susan swing herself up into a tree, followed by a huge grey wolf,
snapping and snarling at her feet.

Peter did not feel very brave, but he rushed straight up to the wolf and aimed a slash
of his sword at its side. Quick as lightning it turned on him. After a short hard fight,
Peter managed to plunge his sword into its heart. A moment later the wolf lay dead.

"Quick!" shouted Aslan. "Centaurs! Eagles! I see another wolf. He will be going to
his mistress. Now is your chance to find the Witch and rescue the fourth Son of Adam."
Instantly a dozen of the swiftest creatures disappeared into the gathering darkness.

Peter shakily wiped his sword clean on the grass.

"Hand it to me and kneel, Son of Adam," said Aslan. Then Aslan struck him with the flat of the blade and said, "Rise up, Sir Peter, Wolf's-Bane."

After Edmund had been made to walk further than he had thought possible, the Witch at last halted in a dark valley. At that moment a wolf rushed up to them, snarling, "They are all at the Stone Table. They have killed my captain. Fly! Fly!"

"No," said the Witch. "Summon all our people. Call out the giants, the ghouls, the ogres and the werewolves. We will fight!"

Edmund found himself being forced to his feet by the dwarf, and roughly tied to a tree. The Witch muttered, "Four thrones in Cair Paravel – but how would it be if only three were filled?"

Edmund heard the awful sound of a knife being sharpened.

Then suddenly there was a drumming of hoofs and beating of wings, and Edmund felt himself being untied. Strong arms were round him and kind voices said, "Steady now," and "Who's got the Witch? Do you mean she's escaped?" For, to their surprise, the Witch had vanished. But just at that moment, Edmund fainted.

Presently the creatures all set off back to the Stone Table, carrying Edmund with them.

When the other children woke up next morning they saw Aslan and Edmund walking together. No one knew what Aslan said to Edmund, but it was a conversation that he never forgot. As the others drew near Edmund shook hands with each of them and said, "I'm sorry," and everyone said, "That's all right."

Then a leopard came up to Aslan and told him there was a message from the enemy.

On to the hilltop came the Witch's dwarf. "The Queen of Narnia desires to come and speak with you," he announced.

"Tell your mistress that I grant her safe conduct – but she must leave her wand behind her at that great oak," replied Aslan.

A few minutes later the White Witch stood before Aslan.

"You have a traitor there, Aslan," she said – everyone knew she meant Edmund – "and the Deep Magic says that for every treachery I have a right to a kill, otherwise Narnia will perish in fire and water."

"It is very true," said Aslan solemnly.

Then he and the Witch walked away from the others and talked, the golden face next to the dead-white one. It was a terrible time this, for everyone, waiting and wondering.

At last the Witch left, with a look of fierce joy on her face.

As soon as she had gone, Aslan said, "We must move from here." So they all set off, and as they walked Aslan outlined to Peter plans for the battle.

That night they camped in a valley, but after everyone had gone to sleep, Susan and Lucy lay awake, talking in the darkness, for Aslan had seemed sad all evening.

"Look!" Susan suddenly said, and they saw the great Lion walking away into the wood. Silently, they both got up and followed him.

In a moonlit clearing he turned to them.

"Dear Aslan, wherever you're going, may we come with you?" the girls begged him.

"Yes," he answered. "I would be glad of your company tonight, if you will promise to stop when I tell you."

Presently they found themselves going up the slope of the hill on which the Stone Table stood. At the edge of the trees Aslan stopped and said, "Children, you must leave me to go on alone. And whatever happens do not let yourselves be seen. Farewell."

The girls cried bitterly, and clung to him for a moment.

A great crowd of evil creatures was standing all round the Stone Table, and in the middle of them was the Witch herself.

"The fool has come!" she cried. "Bind him fast."

Shouting and jeering, they tied the Lion with tight cords. It took all their efforts to lift him on to the table. Susan and Lucy waited for Aslan to roar and spring at his enemies, but he didn't, and they realised with horror that he was sacrificing himself for Edmund.

The Witch raised her stone knife with a cruel laugh. As she struck, the girls couldn't bear to look and covered their eyes.

For a few moments the girls were in danger, as with wild cries the vile creatures came sweeping off the hilltop and disappeared into the forest.

Lucy and Susan crept out on to the open hill-top. They knelt sobbing in the wet grass and kissed the dead Aslan's cold face.

All night long they kept watch over him. Then, as they watched the sun rise, they heard a great cracking, deafening noise behind them. The Stone Table was broken in two – and Aslan had gone.

"Oh, is it more magic?" cried Susan.

"Yes!" said a great voice behind their backs. There, larger than ever, stood Aslan himself.

"Aren't you dead then, dear Aslan?" said Lucy.

He stooped his golden head and licked her forehead, and both girls flung themselves upon him.

"You see," he told them, "there is a magic even older than the Deep Magic. It says that if an innocent victim was killed instead of a traitor, the Table would crack, and Death start working backwards. Oh, children, I feel my strength coming back to me." And he roared.

Then Aslan told Lucy and Susan to climb on to his back, for they had a long way to go.

They sped through orchards of snow-white cherry trees, past roaring waterfalls and down into wild valleys.

It was nearly midday when they found themselves at the Witch's castle. Aslan made a flying leap right over the castle wall and Susan and Lucy tumbled gently off his back, in the middle of a courtyard full of statues.

Then Aslan bounded up to a stone lion and
breathed on him. A streak of gold ran along
his marble back, and as the colour spread,
the lion shook his mane and the heavy stone
folds rippled into living hair.

Everywhere he went, Aslan brought the statues to life, and
the whole place rang with shouts and laughter. Best of all was
when Lucy found Mr Tumnus.

Then the giant, Rumblebuffin, knocked down part of the castle
wall, and everyone set off for the battle to help Peter and the others.

When they arrived, there were statues dotted all over the battlefield – the Witch had clearly been using her wand. With a roar that shook all Narnia, Aslan flung himself upon her.

Most of the enemy was killed in the first charge, and when the rest saw that the Witch was dead, they either gave up or fled.

Peter looked pale, and much older. He told the girls how Edmund had fought his way through three ogres to the Witch, and smashed his sword down on her wand. But he had been badly hurt.

Remembering her precious cordial, Lucy poured a few drops into her brother's mouth. In moments he was healed, and there on the battlefield Aslan made him a knight.

The next day, they all marched eastward, to Cair Paravel.

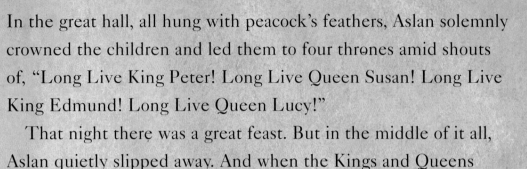

In the great hall, all hung with peacock's feathers, Aslan solemnly crowned the children and led them to four thrones amid shouts of, "Long Live King Peter! Long Live Queen Susan! Long Live King Edmund! Long Live Queen Lucy!"

That night there was a great feast. But in the middle of it all, Aslan quietly slipped away. And when the Kings and Queens noticed that he wasn't there they said nothing about it for, as Mr Beaver had warned them, "He'll be coming and going. He's wild, you know. Not like a *tame* lion."

And so the years passed. Peter, Susan, Edmund and Lucy reigned over Narnia well and were loved by all.

Then one day Mr Tumnus brought them news that the White Stag, who could grant wishes, had been seen in the Western Woods. So the two Kings and the two Queens set out on a hunting party.

As soon as they entered the thick wood Queen Susan said, "How strange – I see a tree of iron." And as they walked towards it, they all suddenly remembered that it was a lamp-post. Soon, to their surprise, they were making their way not through branches but through coats.

Next moment they all came tumbling out of a wardrobe into an empty room, and they were no longer Kings and Queens but just Peter, Susan, Edmund and Lucy in their old clothes. It was the very same hour of the very same day on which they had all gone into the wardrobe to hide.

And when they went to explain to the Professor why four of the coats out of his wardrobe were missing, he didn't tell them not to be silly but believed the whole story.

"You won't get into Narnia again through the wardrobe," he said. "But some day you will get back. Once a King or Queen in Narnia, always a King or Queen in Narnia!"

And that is the very end of the adventure of the wardrobe. But if the Professor was right, it was only the beginning of the adventures of Narnia.